D0688312

OLIVIA™
Sells Cookies

adapted by Natalie Shaw
based on the screenplay "Olivia's Good Luck" written by Jill Gorey and Barbara Herndon
illustrated by Patrick Spaziante

Simon Spotlight
New York   London   Toronto   Sydney   New Delhi

Based on the TV series OLIVIA™ as seen on Nickelodeon™

SIMON SPOTLIGHT
An imprint of Simon & Schuster Children's Publishing Division
1230 Avenue of the Americas, New York, New York 10020
OLIVIA™ Ian Falconer Ink Unlimited, Inc. and © 2013 Ian Falconer and Classic Media, LLC
All rights reserved, including the right of reproduction in whole or in part in any form.
SIMON SPOTLIGHT and colophon are registered trademarks of Simon & Schuster, Inc.
For information about special discounts for bulk purchases, please contact Simon & Schuster Special Sales
at 1-866-506-1949 or business@simonandschuster.com.
Manufactured in the United States of America 1112 LAK
First Edition 1 2 3 4 5 6 7 8 9 10
ISBN 978-1-4424-5965-6
ISBN 978-1-4424-5966-3 (eBook)

It was time for breakfast, but Olivia was too busy to sit down.

"Has anyone seen my lucky tights?" Olivia asked.

"Don't look at me. I don't even know what tights are," said Ian.

Olivia explained that her lucky tights were stretchy and had red and white stripes.

"Let me check. Maybe I put them on by accident," replied Olivia's dad, making her mom laugh.

"Honey, you have a drawer full of tights," Mother said.

"But they're not lucky tights," Olivia explained. "They won't help me run faster, or jump higher, or . . ."

Olivia stopped talking when she saw William crawling into the kitchen, pulling his baby blanket along with him.

"There they are!" said Olivia. "They're stuck on William's blanket!"

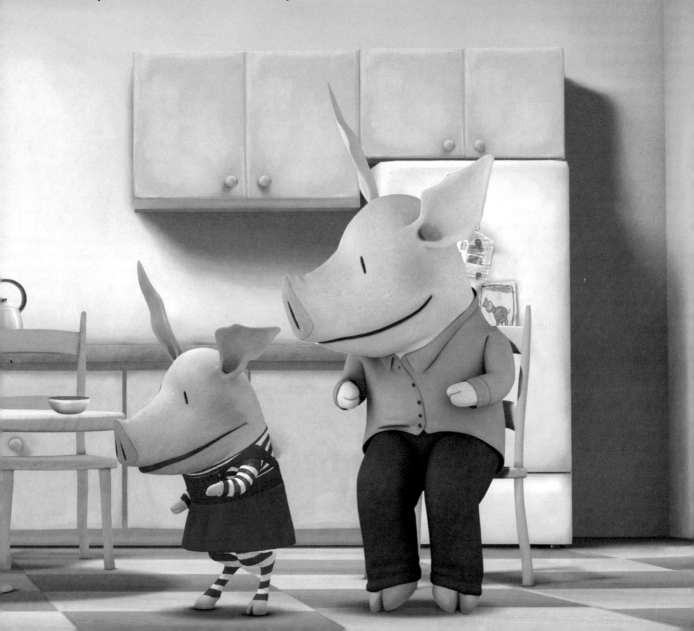

Later at school it was time for show-and-tell. Olivia asked to go first.
"These are my lucky tights," Olivia said. "They help me do amazing things!"
"What do you mean?" asked Mrs. Hoggenmuller.

Olivia imagined that she was the star performer in the circus.
"Presenting Olivia, and her lucky tights!" said the announcer.
Olivia and her lucky tights rode a unicycle and juggled at the same time. Olivia
bowed as the crowd clapped and gave her a round of applause. . . .

Next it was Francine's turn to show and tell. "This is the trophy I won last year for selling the most cookies of anyone in my Young Pioneers troop!" Francine said. "I got my picture in the paper, too! I'm the best cookie seller ever."

"Well, this year, I'm going to sell the most cookies!" Olivia announced.

"Good luck with that, Olivia," replied Francine. "May the best cookie seller win!"

The next day Olivia told her dad that she was trying to become the best cookie seller ever. "So, how many boxes do you want to buy?" she asked.

"I like your can-do spirit, Olivia!" Father replied.

"I'll buy two boxes."

Olivia was surprised. "Two boxes!
That's it?"

"Honey, we don't need a lot of cookies
in the house," Father said. "Besides, in
order to be a good salesperson you've
got to go out there and sell . . . and not
just to your family."

Julian offered to help sell cookies.

"Thanks, Julian," Olivia said as they walked to the first house. "We'll have to work extra hard to sell cookies today because my lucky tights are missing—again! But I think we can still do it!"

They knocked on Mrs. Casey's door.

"Hello, Olivia and Julian!" Mrs. Casey said. "What can I do for you?"

"Well, Mrs. Casey," answered Olivia, "we're here to sell you some cookies!"

But Mrs. Casey had already bought cookies from Francine. Olivia and Julian thanked her and headed to the next house.

The family next door had already bought cookies from Francine, too, but Olivia and Julian didn't give up. They knocked on the door of the next house, but that neighbor also had a box of cookies.

"Let me guess . . . Francine?" Olivia asked.

Meanwhile, workers were jackhammering the pavement outside, and the loud noise was making William cry.

"Maybe we should find somewhere quieter to sell cookies," suggested Olivia's father.

"How about the grocery store?" Olivia asked.

When they arrived at the grocery store, Olivia was hopeful. "We're going to sell so many cookies!" she said to Julian. "I wonder what Francine will think about my brilliant idea!"

"Why don't you ask her?" said Julian, pointing to Francine.

Sure enough, Francine was selling cookies at the grocery store, too. "Guess what, Olivia? I'm almost sold out," she said with a smile. "You have a lot of catching up to do if you want to be the best cookie seller ever!"

Olivia and her father returned home. Olivia was feeling discouraged.
"I'm sorry you didn't sell more cookies today, honey," Father told Olivia.
"Boy, being a salesperson isn't as easy as I thought it would be!" Olivia said.

Then Olivia's mom walked in, holding William and trying to comfort him.
"William's favorite blanket shrank in the wash and he won't stop crying," said
Mother. "So I thought maybe he would like this little bear."
"Waaah!" cried William, throwing the bear behind the couch.

Olivia went to pick up the little bear and saw something else behind the couch. It was her lucky tights! William saw the lucky tights, too. He immediately stopped crying.

"Here, William," Olivia said, giving her lucky tights to her baby brother. "I think you need these more than I do."
"Olivia, that's very nice of you to give your lucky tights to William," her mother said. "You're the best big sister ever!"

William cooed and giggled, and there was peace and quiet in the house . . .
until the jackhammering began again outside.
"Those workers have been out there all day," said Mother.
"You're right," said Olivia. And then she had a wonderful idea. "You know,
I bet the workers are really hungry!"

Olivia ran outside and sold the rest of her cookies to the construction workers. "I don't think I sold the *most* cookies, but at least I sold all my boxes," she told her family. "And I even did it without my lucky tights!"

"Nice work, Olivia!" her dad said.

That night at bedtime Olivia handed a stack of books to her mom. "Usually, when I wear my lucky tights, you read four books to me at bedtime," she explained. Mother and Father agreed, since the lucky tights were the only thing that kept William from crying.

"My lucky tights are even luckier than I thought," Olivia whispered, but it had been a long day, and soon she was fast asleep.